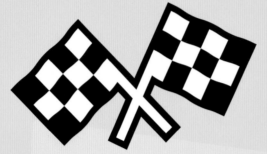

This Roary The Racing Car
Annual 2010 belongs to

....

First published in Great Britain by
HarperCollins Children's Books in 2009
1 3 5 7 9 10 8 6 4 2
ISBN: 978-0-00-732549-8

Based on the television series Roary the Racing Car
© Chapman Entertainment & David Jenkins 2009

Visit Roary at www.roarytheracingcar.com

Printed and bound in China

Hi, I'm Roary and this is Big Chris! Welcome to Silver Hatch!
Roary's won lots of trophies from coming first in races, but we've lost nine of them in this annual. Can you help us to find them?

Contents

1

The Gang's Here!

Drive your pen or pencil over the dots to see who is at the track today!

Drifter

James

Maxi

Tin Top

88

Loada

Nick

Flash in the Pan

Flash was busy in his underground burrow, deep beneath the tree at Hare-Pin Bend. He'd spent all morning working on his skateboard.

"Gotta oil the wheels and shine the foot deck," he muttered. "That way it'll go even faster!"

Flash dreamed of beating Roary and his friends in a lap round Silver Hatch. His skateboard was nippy, but unfortunately it was no match for the racing cars.

"If only I could take a short cut to get ahead," he sighed.

Suddenly the rabbit grinned, his eyes twinkling with a naughty idea.

Flash pulled up at the workshop with a screech.

"Morning Roary!" he called.

The red single seater was sitting on the ramp, waiting for Big Chris to give him an oil change.

"Hello Flash," beeped Roary. "What are you up to?"

The rabbit pointed to the empty track. "Fancy a race later?"

Roary revved his engine. "You bet!"

Just then, Big Chris walked in carrying a large oil can. Flash grabbed his board and scooted out the door.

"Meet you lunchtime," he waved. "Gotta dash!"

11

Roary felt excited about the race all morning, but things got even better when Marsha arrived.

"Gather round everybody!" she cried. "I've got some news."

Big Chris turned off his radio while Roary parked up next to Maxi and the others.

"Mr Carburettor would like you to do a practice session on a skid pan this afternoon," announced Marsha.

"What's a skid pan?" asked Roary, feeling a bit silly.

"Good question, lad!" said Big Chris. "It's a special section of track that's been made all slippery."

"Swerving on a skid pan is a great way to test your driving skills," said Marsha.

Big Chris nodded. "After lunch I'm going to prepare the road through Flat-Out Forest with a mixture of oil and water."

"You'll need to take it very carefully," warned Marsha. "We don't want any accidents out there."

Maxi and Roary couldn't wait to test their tyres on the skid pan.

"Let's do it!"

Back at Hare-Pin Bend, Flash couldn't wait to take on the racing cars.

"Rather you than me," sighed Molecom. "Those cars are super-speedy." Flash giggled. "Not a problem. Just you wait and see!"

While the cars were busy at the workshop, Flash tiptoed out on to the track.

"I just need to move a few of these cones," he sniggered. "And I'll be race-ready!"

The sneaky rabbit diverted the route so that the cars would be sent on a complete lap of the course.

"While Roary and Maxi motor round Silver Hatch," smirked Flash. "I'll take a short cut through Flat-Out Forest."

By midday, Big Chris's tummy was rumbling. He had spent all morning getting the skid pan slippery for the practice session.

"Right then!" he said. "I'm off for a doughnut or two before we get started."

Flash waited until Big Chris had climbed into Rusty before skating over to the racing cars.

"Ready for that race now?" he asked. Roary didn't need to be asked twice. "Light 'em up!" he grinned. "Beating you round the track will get us warmed up nicely for our skid pan session."

15

Flash broke into a toothy grin as he watched Roary, Maxi, Cici, Drifter and Tin Top all motor up to the starter's grid.

"First one back round to the start is the winner!" he called.

"Mamma mia!" Maxi pulled down his sunglasses and revved his engine. "This is going to be too easy."

Molecom was put in charge of starting the race. "Lights out!"

As soon as the flag went down the racers sped off. The cars broke away on to the open track, but Flash wasn't worried – he had a plan.

16

Roary was in pole position, but Maxi and Cici were right behind him.

"Flash gotta dash!" chuckled the rabbit, turning his skateboard off the main track.

While the cars fought it out on the course, Flash moved back the safety cones and got ready to cut through Flat-Out Forest.

"I'll make it back to the finish in no time," he laughed.

Up at Dinkie's Corner, Roary looked over his shoulder for a sign of Flash. He knew he could beat him, but he thought the race would be closer than this!

Suddenly Roary put on the brakes. "Maybe Flash is in trouble?"

The kind-hearted car waited for the others to catch up, then turned round to find the missing rabbit.

"Skid my skateboard!" cried Flash. "What's happened to this road?"

The rabbit skidded from left to right, his wheels sliding on the slippery track. Just then Roary screeched up beside him.

"Flash!" he shouted. "Your cheating has led you straight on to the skid pan!"

Flash turned back to see Maxi and the others behind him.

They looked very cross.

"You found my short cut!" cried the rabbit. "And now I-I can't stop!"

"There's only one thing for it," said Roary, turning his wheels towards the safety tyres piled up on the side of the track.

"Turn into the tyres Flash," yelled Maxi. "Now!"

Flash did as he was told.

"Yikes!" he cried, as his skateboard crashed headlong into the safety cones. The rabbit was sent flying across the track before landing with a bump on the mound of tumbled tyres.

The cars slowed down and wheeled over to Flash.

"Are you OK?" asked Cici.

The rabbit looked up dizzily, just managing a thumbs-up.

"Thanks Roary," he whispered.

Big Chris and Plugger were on the scene in seconds.

"What's going on here?" he cried. "We were supposed to be doing the skid pan session *after* lunch."

"You'd better ask Flash," sniffed Maxi.

"We were having a race," sighed Flash, looking at the tarmac.

Big Chris put his hands on his hips and frowned. "So what are you doing in Flat-Out Forest?"

"It was just my little short cut," gulped the rabbit. "I didn't know you were going to cover the road with slippery stuff!"

Flash was in trouble, but the cars couldn't help feeling sorry for him. Back at the workshop he admitted everything.

"Silly rabbit," tutted Big Chris. "You could have hurt yourself and the cars."

Flash nodded, then turned to Roary. "How did you find me?"

"When we came looking for you I saw that you'd moved the cones back," said Roary. "It wasn't hard to guess you'd taken a cut-through."

"Thanks for saving me," said Flash. "Sorry."

"Don't worry," grinned Big Chris. "We've got the perfect way for you to make it up to us."

Roary drove forward holding a sponge and a bucket of soapy water. "After we're done on the skid pan – you can clear it up!"

Time to Clear Up!

Colour this picture of Roary and Flash getting ready to clean the slippery track.

22

Cone Maze

Oh no! Flash has rearranged the cones on the track and now the cars don't know where to go! Help them by finding the way through this maze.

Finish

Start

Skid Pan Race

Race around the track like Roary and his friends!
The youngest player goes first. Take turns rolling the die and
moving around the track the number of spaces shown.

17 18 19 20

16 15 14 13

Start

1 2 3 4

24

If you land on an oil can, skid forward on to the next space.

If you land on a cone, miss a turn while you move it out of the way.

You will need:
A die
A playing piece for each player

21 22 23 Finish

12 11 10 9

5 6 7 8

Spot the Difference

Look carefully at these two pictures.
Can you find five differences between them?

Safety First!

Colour this picture of PC Pete and his police car Nick.

The One and Only

Can you find the one item on this page that does not have a double?
Circle it when you are sure.

Rusty Remembers...

Rusty loves to tell the cars about when he had
wheels and travelled the world! Draw him a memory
of one of his exciting trips below.

29

Molecom's Toolbox

Molecom is tidying up, but some of these things don't belong in his toolbox. Circle the things that don't belong to Molecom.

Ready for Anything!

What is Big Chris ready to do? Match the pictures of him with the labels to find out.

1. Ready to sing!

4. Ready for a break.

3. Ready for snow.

2. Ready for bed.

C

A

B

D

33

On the Farm

1. What is Dinkie eating?
2. What colour is Farmer Green's tie?
3. Who has come to visit Farmer Green?

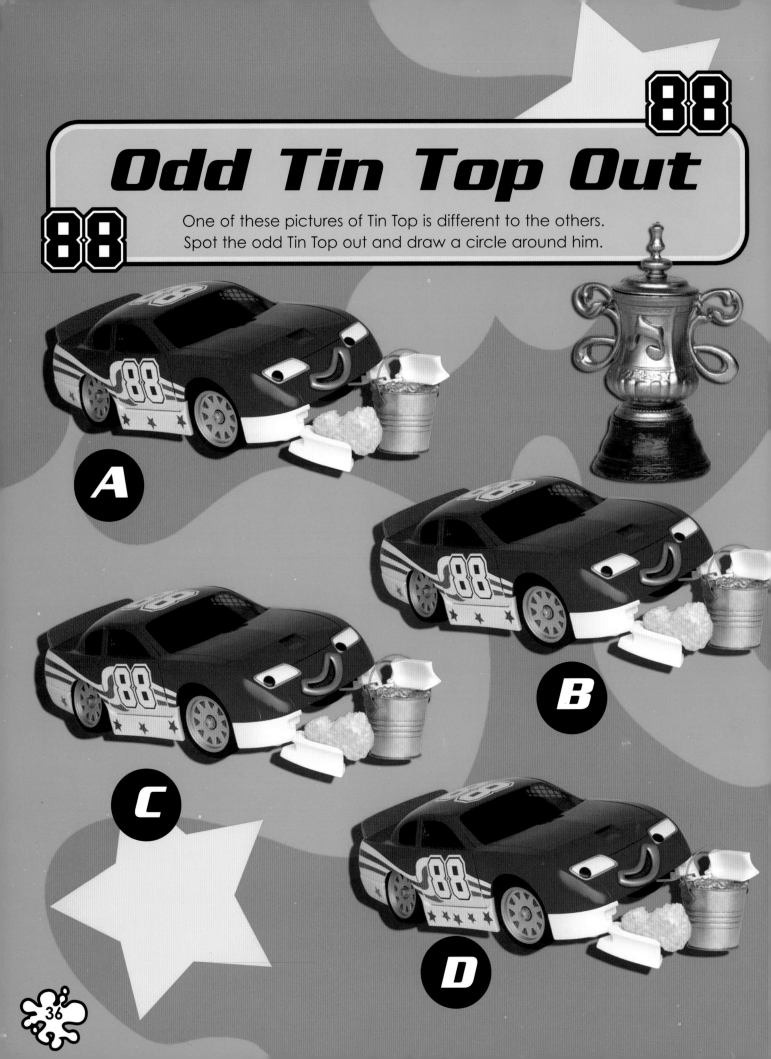

Odd Tin Top Out

One of these pictures of Tin Top is different to the others.
Spot the odd Tin Top out and draw a circle around him.

A

B

C

D

Cone Count

Flash has crashed and sent these cones flying!
Can you help him count how many there are?

Write your answer here:

Muddy Maxi

88

It was Sunday morning and Marsha had arrived at Silver Hatch extra early.

"Cooee!" she called, knocking on Rusty's door. "Big Chris?"

There was a groan from inside, then the sleepy mechanic stuck his head out.

"Hello Marsha," said Big Chris. "What time do you call this?"

Marsha checked her watch. "Getting up time I should say. Mr Carburettor is going to be here in one hour."

She jumped back on Zippee and fastened her helmet.

"But I'm still in my pyjamas!" groaned Big Chris.

"Meet you at the workshop in five," called Marsha. "We need the place to be spotless!"

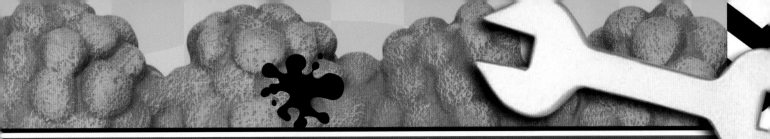

Big Chris grabbed a slice of toast and a mug of tea, then headed out to the workshop.

"Wakey wakey you lot," he grinned, switching on the lights.

As soon as Roary and the other cars heard that Mr Carburettor was coming, they beeped their horns and flashed their headlights.

"He must have some news," decided Maxi. "Perhaps I'm due for a re-fit."

A little while later, Hellie touched down outside. Everyone waited as Mr Carburettor stepped on to the tarmac.

"Morning my Maxi!" beamed Mr Carburettor as he walked into the workshop. "How's my Formula 1 star?"

"Tip-top, thank you," said Maxi, revving his engine proudly.

Marsha beckoned the cars forward. "Mr Carburettor has got an announcement to make."

"I'm entering a Silver Hatch team in the Southern Championships," announced Mr Carburettor. "My two fastest cars will be transported there in Loada next weekend."

"Wow!" gasped Roary. "That's the biggest race of the year!"

Maxi nodded. "And I'm odds-on to win it."

Mr Carburettor pulled out a handkerchief and gave Maxi's yellow bodywork a little polish.

"I'm sure you will my bambino," he gushed. "You're the fastest car on the grid."

Roary closed his eyes and imagined himself winning the Southern Championship trophy.

"I wish I could race in an awesome event like that," he sighed.

"Maybe you will lad," said Big Chris. "Mr Carburettor's holding time trials this morning."

"The quickest pair to complete three laps of the track gets a place in Loada," nodded the racetrack boss.

The cars headed out to the starter's grid.

"I don't know why I'm bothering with this," boasted Maxi. "Everybody knows that I'm the fastest car in Silver Hatch."

"Good luck Roary," said Cici. "Give it your best shot."

Roary grinned, then set his eyes on the road. "You too. Now let's go!"

As soon as the flag went down all the cars rumbled off the grid.

"Go on my son!" yelled Big Chris. "You can do it Roary!"

The racing was fast and furious. The cars screeched round bends and tore through tunnels, battling each other for first place.

By the second lap, Maxi had pulled ahead.

"This is too easy," he laughed, cruising down a straight.

"Time to move up a gear!" shouted Roary, pushing himself forward.

"Race you!" cried Cici.

The little stunt car overtook Maxi and Roary then zoomed at top speed towards the next corner. Suddenly she slid into a spin, crashing off the side of the track.

"Uh-oh, I'm out!" she frowned.

"Bad luck Cici!" shouted Roary, slamming on the brakes.

"Plugger's on his way," added Tin Top.

Roary swerved to pass his friend, but it was too late. The car was sent spinning towards the crash barrier, with Maxi hurtling behind him. The out-of-control pair finally came to a halt in a muddy field.

"Ugh," snapped Maxi. "Look at my paintwork!"

Both cars were covered in dirt, but that didn't bother Roary. He quickly did a U-turn then zoomed back towards the track.

"Got to get back in the race!" he cried.

While the other cars raced on, Maxi pulled on his hand brake.

"I can't win looking like this!" he cried. "My shine is ruined!"

Big Chris drove up in Plugger.

"What's up lad?" he asked. "Have you over-heated?"

"Much worse," replied Maxi, turning up his nose. "Get this mud off me now!"

The mechanic grinned, then reached for his bucket and sponge.

"What about the race?" he asked.

"That can wait," said Maxi. "I'll beat them in a minute."

45

Maxi insisted on a wash with soapy water plus a full wax and polish. By the time Big Chris had finished, the other racing cars were already on their third lap.

"Right!" puffed Big Chris. "Are you satisfied now?"

While Maxi checked his wing mirrors, he heard a woooosh in the distance.

"What was that?" asked the Formula 1 car.

Big Chris pointed to the track. "That, my son, was the sound of you being lapped."

"Mamma Mia!"

Maxi roared back on to the track, revving his engine as hard as he could. The other cars were so far ahead now he couldn't even see them.

"I gotta win this race!" he shouted. "Mr Carburettor is watching!"

Finally Drifter came into view. Maxi changed gears and got ready to overtake.

"Time to fire it up!" decided Drifter, switching on his rocket-powered reserve booster.

With a blaze of power, the street-car shot off into the distance.

As he approached the final straight, Roary was firing on all gaskets.

"Come on, Roary," he said to himself. "You can do this!"

Seeing Cici cheering from the pit lane gave him the energy for one last push.

"You've done it!" bellowed Big Chris, waving the chequered flag.

"But where is my Maxi?" asked Mr Carburettor.

Big Chris clapped Drifter and Tin Top as they cruised into second and third place. "Looks like he's coming in fourth!"

The Silver Hatch team waited for Maxi to skid round to the finishing line.

"What a day," he groaned. "I think I'm having a breakdown!"

"I'm sorry Maxi," said Mr Carburettor. "But I'll be taking Roary and Drifter to the Southern Championships."

Roary gave Drifter a happy high-five.

"We won't let Silver Hatch down!" he promised.

Big Chris patted Maxi fondly. "Let's get you back to the workshop son. Maybe next time you'll think twice before choosing to be too big for your bonnet."

Take it to the Maxi!

Maxi loves to be clean and shiny! Colour this picture of him getting ready to race.

MAXI™

DGAX

Trophy Time

Roary dreams of winning the Southern Championship trophy! What do you think it would look like? Draw it below.

Here Comes Hellie!

Hellie is flying to Silver Hatch with Mr Carburettor, but it's a really cloudy day. Help Marsha direct him safely through the maze to land.

Start

Finis

Spanner Search

The word spanner appears in this grid seven times.
It could be across, up, down or diagonally. Can you find them all?

S	P	A	N	N	E	R	W	Y	H
P	P	O	N	Q	T	R	U	N	V
A	M	A	S	P	A	N	N	E	R
N	S	L	N	D	S	A	T	G	E
N	H	P	O	N	L	P	B	H	N
E	Q	W	A	R	E	T	Y	I	N
R	O	K	L	N	H	R	N	B	A
V	C	X	A	S	N	D	F	G	P
I	K	L	P	U	Y	E	E	D	S
W	S	P	A	N	N	E	R	L	G

53

Life's a Breeze!

Roary and Cici are visiting Breeze down at the beach.
Which of the smaller pictures can you find in the bigger one?

54

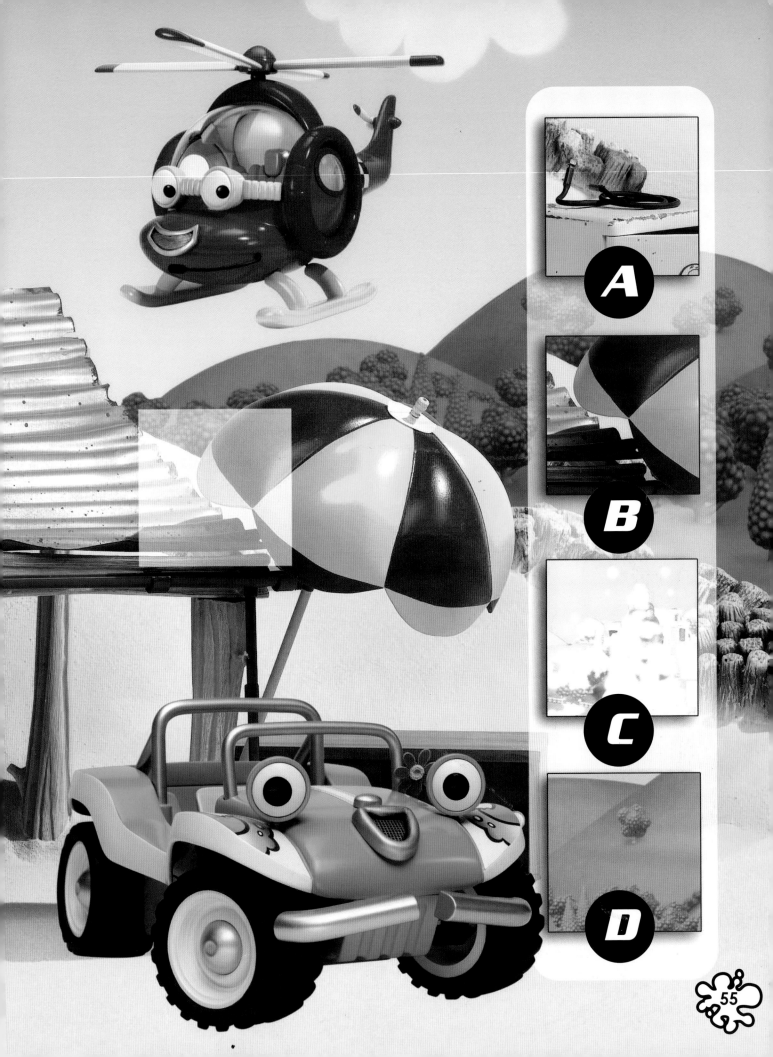

A

B

C

D

55

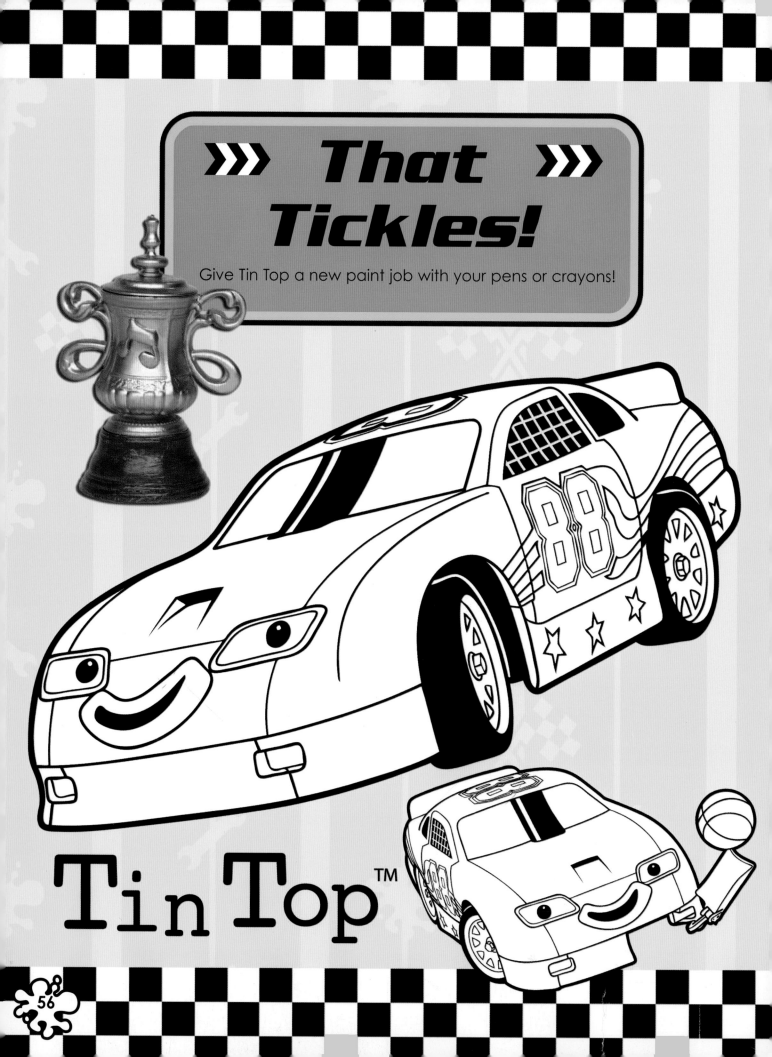

That Tickles!

Give Tin Top a new paint job with your pens or crayons!

88

TinTop™

Big Chris's Feast

Big Chris loves pizza and doughnuts! Draw a tasty topping for his pizza and decorate his doughnuts with lots of colourful sprinkles!

57

What Can You Remember?

It's been great racing with you through this annual, but how much can you remember? Answer these questions to find out. Write your answers in the boxes.

1. What did Big Chris put on the track to make it all slippery?

A   B   C

2. Who was not covered in snow?

A   B   C

3. What was Dinkie eating on the farm?
A. An apple.
B. A banana.
C. A carrot.

4. How many cones did you count with Flash?
A. Ten.
B. Eleven.
C. Nine.

5. Who got to go to the Southern Championship?

A   B   C

6. What topping did you draw on Big Chris's pizza?

Answers

Page 23 Cone Maze

Page 26 Spot the Difference

Page 28 The One and Only

Page 30 Snow Shapes
A. Breeze, B. Cici, C. Loada, D. Drifter.

Page 32 Molecom's Toolbox

Page 33 Ready for Anything!
A. 3, B. 1, C. 2, D. 4.

Page 34 On the Farm
A. Dinkie is eating a carrot.
B. Farmer Green's tie is red.
C. Big Chris has come to visit
Farmer Green.

Page 36 Odd Tin Top Out
D is the odd one out.

Page 37 Cone Count
There are eleven cones.

Answers

Page 52 Here Comes Hellie!

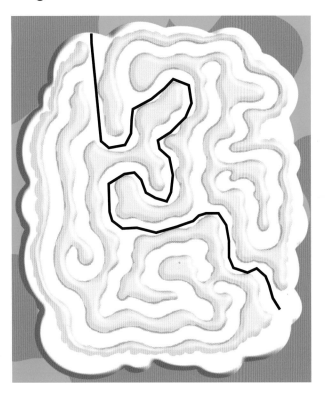

Page 53 Spanner Search

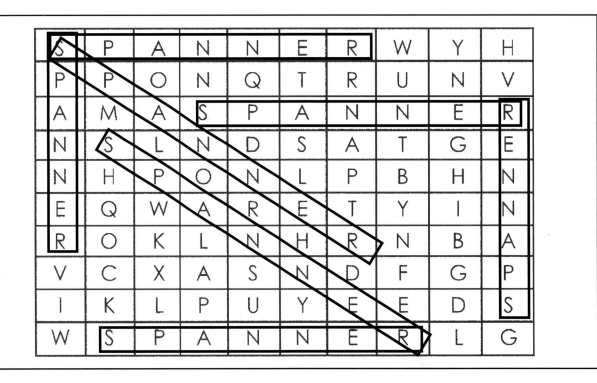

Page 54 Life's a Breeze

Page 58 What Can You Remember?
1. B, 2. A, 3. C, 4. B, 5. C.

Hidden Trophies
The nine hidden trophies are on pages 9, 22, 24, 26, 29, 36, 40, 49, 56

ROARY The Racing Car MAGAZINE

FREE! Spinning click clack flag

Plus over 50 stickers and workbook inside!

➤ Puzzles to do!
➤ Games to play!
➤ Stories to read!
➤ On sale every 4 weeks from your local newsagent!

LET'S GO!

Help us tidy up Silver Hatch

Play my racing board game

Lead Dinkie through maze

➤ Meet PC Pete and Nick!

FREE GIFT EVERY ISSUE!

SUBSCRIBE and SAVE!

SUBSCRIBE NOW FOR ONLY £11.60 FOR 6 ISSUES, SAVING 10%!

For more details and to subscribe, call 0844 844 0262 (overseas +44 (0)1795 414 809) quoting ROANNUAL or go online and enter the code at www.titantots.com

TitanTOTs

Check out our other great pre-school magazines...